I SURVIVED

THE *HINDENBURG* DISASTER, 1937

by Lauren Tarshis

illustrated by Scott Dawson

Scholastic Inc.

Text copyright © 2016 by Lauren Tarshis

Illustrations copyright © 2016 by Scholastic Inc.

Photo of the *Hindenburg* on page iv © Popperfoto/Getty Images

Photo of the *Hindenburg* on page 103 © STR/AP Images

All rights reserved. Published by Scholastic Inc., *Publishers since 1920*.

SCHOLASTIC and associated logos are trademarks and/or

registered trademarks of Scholastic Inc.

ISBN 978-0-545-65850-8

10 9 8 7 6 5 4 3 2 1   16 17 18 19 20

Printed in the U.S.A.   40

First printing, March 2016

Designed by Yaffa Jaskoll

Series design by Tim Hall

To Nancy Mercado,
with gratitude and love

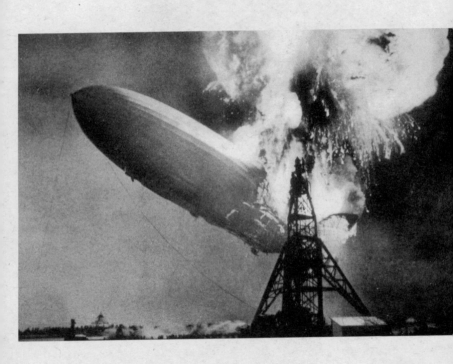

CHAPTER 1

THURSDAY, MAY 6, 1937
7:25 P.M.
LAKEHURST, NEW JERSEY

In seconds, the *Hindenburg* would explode. The greatest flying machine ever built would burst into flames. It would crash to the ground in a heap of twisted metal and smoldering ash.

Just minutes before, eleven-year-old Hugo Ballard had been standing at the airship's huge windows. After a three-day journey across the Atlantic, the *Hindenburg* was about to land.

1

But then came the massive explosion.

Kaboom!

On the ground, hundreds of people had gathered to watch the landing. Now they stared in horror as the great airship erupted into a massive fireball.

And inside the crippled airship, Hugo was in a fight for his life.

The force of the explosive blast sent him flying back. He landed on the ground with a sickening thud. Frantic people fell on top of him, and he was nearly crushed.

Someone's heavy shoe kicked his face. An elbow jabbed him in the eye. A knee pressed against his throat, making it impossible to breathe.

He managed to free himself, but now the flames were everywhere. Poisonous black smoke rushed up his nose and down his throat. Tears gushed from his burning eyes. Red-hot drops of molten metal rained down, burning through his clothes and sizzling against his skin.

But Hugo barely noticed the pain. He just wanted to find his parents and his little sister, Gertie. He cried out for them, but his words were

smothered by the terrible noises all around —
screams of pain and panic, the shattering of
glass, the crackle and roar of the flames. People
smashed windows and leaped out, their terrified
cries echoing as they fell through the fiery sky.

Hugo clawed his way across the floor, gasping
for breath. The searing heat blistered his hands
and knees.

He could feel the airship falling, falling, falling.
Any second it would crash to the ground.

The *Hindenburg* was doomed.

And so, it seemed, was Hugo.

CHAPTER 2

Hugo held his four-year-old sister, Gertie, tightly in his arms. They were standing in the airport waiting room. Within the hour, they'd be flying to America on the *Hindenburg*. Now they just had to have their bags inspected by the mean-looking German guards.

"No matches or lighters will be permitted on the *Hindenburg*!" a soldier barked out in English and German.

The guards talked in a way that made every word sound like a curse.

"Why are they so worried about matches?" Mom asked nervously.

Mom wasn't the jittery type — she'd shoo a deadly snake from their kitchen as if it were a ladybug. But none of them had ever flown before. And the idea of rising more than six hundred feet into the sky and then flying across the Atlantic Ocean was making her nervous.

Dad gave Mom a pat on the arm. "It's just because the *Hindenburg* is powered by hydrogen gas. It's very flammable."

"Please don't remind me," Mom said, looking queasy.

Dad put an arm around Mom's shoulders and pulled her close.

"You don't have to worry," he said. "The Germans have a perfect safety record with their zeppelins. Right, Hugo?"

He shot Hugo a look that said, *I need some help here*.

"It's true, Mom," Hugo chimed in. He'd learned all he could about the *Hindenburg* and its sister ship, the *Graf Zeppelin*. Now he tried to remember some of the amazing facts he'd read.

"The *Hindenburg* made thirty-four trips across the Atlantic last year," he said, using his most expert voice. "And the *Graf Zeppelin* has flown more than a million miles without one problem. Really, Mom. The *Hindenburg* is the safest way to travel."

Mom perked up a little bit.

"That's good," she said. "But I'd still rather be on a nice big ship."

"Like the *Titanic*?" Dad said, raising an eyebrow.

Who could forget the celebrated ocean liner that had hit an iceberg and sunk twenty-five years ago?

Mom frowned, but Dad had made a good point. Thousands of people had died in shipwrecks over the years. And not one person had been killed on a German passenger airship.

Of course, there had been some grisly accidents on *military* airships over the years — fiery explosions and deadly crashes. The most terrible was the disaster of a U.S. Navy airship that had happened just a few years ago. The *Akron* had been flying off the coast of New Jersey when it was swept into a violent thunderstorm. It crashed into the ocean and more than seventy men were killed.

But German airships, known as zeppelins, were different. They were famous for their safety. German pilots were the very best in the world. Hugo really didn't have the slightest worry about the *Hindenburg.*

What he was worried about, as usual, was his little sister.

Gertie wasn't feeling so well today. And now she was all teary over their dog, Panya. It turned out dogs weren't allowed in the passenger areas of the *Hindenburg.* A few minutes ago, a member of the zeppelin's crew had come to take their little mutt away. Panya would spend the voyage in the *Hindenburg*'s cargo hold.

Hugo didn't know who howled louder when Panya was carried off — the dog or Gertie.

Gertie looked at Hugo.

"I miss Panya," she said, her lip trembling.

"I have an idea," Hugo said, straightening one of Gertie's curly pigtails. "Let's go look at the zeppelin."

If anything could get Gertie's mind off Panya, it was the *Hindenburg*.

CHAPTER 3

Hugo's plan worked.

Gertie's blue eyes popped open as they stared out the window at the massive zeppelin. It sat on its airfield, tied down by thick white ropes. It reminded Hugo of a spectacular beast, with metal bones showing through silver skin.

But Gertie had a different idea.

"Oogo, it looks like a giant sausage!"

Hugo laughed; she had a point.

But that giant sausage happened to be the biggest airship ever built. At least a hundred crewmen scurried around it. The zeppelin was so huge that the men looked like flies buzzing around an elephant.

Hugo gave Gertie a little lesson about zeppelins. Some people called them airships or dirigibles, he explained, but he liked the word *zeppelin*. The word was actually the name of the brilliant man who figured out how to get these huge airships to fly, Count Ferdinand von Zeppelin.

Hugo pointed out the little car that hung from the bottom of the zeppelin, right behind its nose.

That was the control car, the *Hindenburg*'s cockpit, where the captain and his crew steered the ship. The passenger compartment was just behind, tucked into the ship's belly.

Gertie turned to Hugo. "Where are its wings?"

"It doesn't need them," he explained. "It's filled up with gas — a special kind of air — that makes it rise into the sky."

"Like a balloon," Gertie said happily.

"Yes," Hugo said, even though that wasn't really right. The *Hindenburg*'s sausage body was actually made of a very light metal. And then the metal frame was covered with a strong fabric. But Gertie was close enough.

Hugo pointed out the four powerful engines that were bolted to the *Hindenburg*'s body. Once the *Hindenburg* was in the air, the engines would rev up, and giant propellers would push the airship forward.

"Oogo, are we really going to fly?" Gertie asked.

"We are," Hugo said, barely believing it himself.

11

Just three weeks before, they'd been thousands of miles away, in the East African country of Kenya. They'd moved there from New York City a year ago. Mom and Dad were science professors. They had always wanted to study the lions in Kenya's Thika Valley. For years it was just a dream. And then eighteen months ago, Mom's aunt Sylvie died, leaving Mom her life's savings. It wasn't a fortune, but it was more than enough to pay for a year or so in Kenya.

"It will be a family adventure," Mom had said.

And what an adventure it had turned out to be.

From their front porch, they could watch herds of zebras and giraffes strolling through the high golden grass. At night, roars of lions echoed through the darkness.

"And good night to *you*!" Gertie would holler back at them.

Sure, at first Hugo missed his pals and his school and his beloved Yankees. But somehow he was never lonely. He had Gertie to chase after. There was the one-eared baboon that came to visit Hugo every day while he did his schoolwork on the porch. And then there was Panya, the ragged mutt that showed up at their door one day and refused to leave. He was a little guy — *panya* means *mouse* in the African language Swahili. But that mousy dog had the brave heart of a lion. He was Gertie and Hugo's fiercest protector.

Hugo had seen more in this past year than most people see in their whole lives. He'd watched twenty-foot pythons climbing up trees and mother crocodiles carrying their babies in their wide-open jaws. He'd seen that one-eared baboon outsmart an eight-thousand-pound hippo.

But Hugo had never seen anything like the *Hindenburg*.

The zeppelin was known around the world. The *Hindenburg* was as famous as Hugo's favorite Yankee, Lou Gehrig. But never had Hugo imagined that he'd have the chance to fly on a zeppelin. His New York pals would say he was the luckiest kid on the planet.

Hugo felt anything but lucky, though.

Because this trip on the *Hindenburg* wasn't just another family adventure.

They were returning to New York City because Gert was very sick.

Her illness had struck six months ago. One day Gert was her joyful self. And the next morning she could barely move, and her body burned with fever.

Weeks passed, then months, and Gertie didn't get better. The fever would disappear for a few weeks, but then it would come raging back. Twice her fever got so high she almost didn't make it through the night. It turned out Gertie had a bad case of malaria, a disease that came from mosquitoes. Dad had gotten malaria, too. But it was more dangerous for little kids, and Gertie just couldn't get well.

That's why they had come to Germany two weeks ago, to see a famous expert in children's diseases. He had no cure, but he told them about a team of doctors in New York City that had a new kind of medicine. As they were leaving his office, the doctor had pulled Dad aside, and Hugo overheard his whispered warning.

"Get your daughter back to New York as quickly as you can," he'd warned. "You are running out of time."

Now Hugo wrapped his arms a little tighter around his sister and swallowed the lump in his throat.

No, this journey on the *Hindenburg* wasn't for excitement.

It was to save Gert's life.

CHAPTER 4

Gertie dropped off to sleep in Hugo's arms, and Hugo leaned back against the wall. He looked around the room, wondering if he would spot any celebrities. Hugo had seen photos of famous athletes and millionaires posing on the famous airship.

But from what Hugo could see, most people looked like rich businessmen and fancy-looking ladies.

No Yankees, that was for sure.

As he scanned the room, he caught sight of a group of uniformed men standing near the exit. They were Nazi soldiers, the men closest to

Germany's leader, Adolf Hitler. Each man wore a black leather coat with a bloodred band on his left arm. The armbands were decorated with a hooked black cross — a swastika, the symbol of the Nazis.

Hugo shuddered.

Hitler and his Nazis were dangerous, Mom and Dad had said, even evil. And the sight of those men gave Hugo a bad feeling — dark and shadowy — like when he saw hippos lurking in the waters of the Thika River near their farm. The hippos looked tame, with their blubbery bodies and fat noses. But in a blink, the four-ton monsters could explode out of the water and chomp you in half.

Hugo was so deep in his frightening thoughts that at first he didn't notice that Mom and Dad were now standing right in front of him.

Mom smiled at the sight of Gertie sleeping so peacefully.

"The inspection took forever," Dad said. "I'm surprised the guard didn't look inside my ears."

"Sweetheart, what's wrong?" Mom said to

Hugo. "You're pale as a ghost. You look like you just found a cobra in your bed."

Hugo's mind swung from Nazis to the giant snake he'd discovered curled up on his pillow not so long ago. The startled serpent had flared its hood and bared its gleaming fangs as it prepared to leap up and bite Hugo on the neck.

Luckily, Panya had come to the rescue. The little mutt had a bark so strange and ferocious that he could scare away the most fiendish beast.

"Garoo, garoo, garoo, garoo!"

Even now Hugo could still picture the petrified snake as it practically flew out of the room.

"I'm fine," Hugo said. "I just wish we were already in New York."

"Me, too," Dad said. "But we should try to enjoy this voyage. I think it's going to be unforgettable."

Hugo didn't doubt that was true.

CHAPTER 5

They followed a line of passengers onto the airfield. It was drizzling, but the cold rain hadn't stopped a crowd of people from gathering to watch the zeppelin take off. It was like a party, with photographers snapping pictures and a band playing brassy German tunes. The loud music woke up Gertie, who stared in amazement at the *Hindenburg*. It loomed over them like a silver mountain.

A smiling man in a uniform stood in front of a metal staircase. The stairs led up into the belly of the airship.

"Willkommen!" he said. "Welcome!"

They walked up the stairs — and into another world.

To Hugo, it seemed they had entered a fancy hotel from the future.

They found their cabin, which was small and very modern. The sleek bunk beds were made with thick blankets and silky sheets. The sink and desk even folded up and down to make extra room. Hugo had never seen anything like it.

They left their suitcases and coats in the cabin and did a quick tour of the two floors of the small passenger area. They peeked into the dining room. Long tables were set with white cloths and sparkling dishes and flowers that looked as if they'd just been picked from someone's garden. Down the hall was the lounge. On the wall was a hand-painted mural of the world, with zeppelins zipping across the sky.

Hugo wanted to explore every inch of the passenger area. But it was time for the zeppelin to take off. And so they joined a small group of passengers standing along a row of windows. The windows actually slanted down, so they had the perfect view of the action on the airfield. Muscled crewmen were unhooking the ropes that held the zeppelin to the ground.

Hugo hadn't noticed that someone had sat down next to him. It was a girl about his age. She had dark blond hair, round brown eyes, and a face scattered with freckles.

"First time on a zeppelin?" she asked.

"Yes," Hugo answered. "What about you?"

She paused for a few seconds, counting silently on her fingers.

"It's my eighth time," she said.

"Wow!" Hugo said with surprise.

Eight times? This girl must be a millionaire! Each *Hindenburg* ticket cost $450, almost as much as a new car. Hugo guessed that Mom and Dad had used the rest of Aunt Sylvie's money to pay for this trip.

"I'm Martha Singer," the girl said. "But call me Marty."

"Hugo."

"That's my father," she said, pointing across the room to a friendly looking man with puffy hair and round glasses. "He works for the Zeppelin Company. They own the *Hindenburg*."

Hugo's mouth dropped open. "Your dad owns the *Hindenburg*?"

"No." She laughed, but not in a way that made Hugo feel dumb. "He just works for the company, in the American office in New York City. We go to Germany a few times a year."

"And you always take a zeppelin?"

"We do," Marty said. "And every trip I see something different. Last time, I got to see a whole family of dolphins. They leaped up out of the water when we flew over them."

"Maybe they wanted to hitch a ride on the *Hindenburg*," Hugo said.

"Who doesn't?" Marty grinned.

A warm feeling filled Hugo's chest, like when he would sip hot chocolate on a freezing New York day. He tried to remember the last time he talked to a kid his own age. Their house in Kenya was surrounded by wilderness, and the nearest village was twenty miles away. Hugo hadn't made any friends in Kenya, unless you counted the one-eared baboon.

Hugo had the urge to tell Marty all about that baboon — and other things, too.

But now it was Gertie's turn to talk.

She turned to Marty and smiled. "You're pretty! You look like a cheetah."

This was one of Gertie's games, to match a person to the animal he or she looked like.

And Marty seemed very happy to be compared to a curious spotted cat.

"Thank you!" she exclaimed.

She narrowed her eyes and studied Gertie.

"And you look like a gazelle with pigtails."

Gertie's pale face lit up.

Just then a man's voice thundered over the loudspeaker.

"Schiff hauf!"

Up ship!

The men on the airstrip let go of the anchor ropes and leaped backward, away from the zeppelin.

Hugo grabbed hold of Gertie, bracing for a sharp jolt as the zeppelin took flight.

But he didn't feel a thing. Like a feather lifted by the breeze, the great airship rose silently off the earth.

Hugo almost forgot to breathe as the world outside got smaller and smaller. The people on the ground shrank into dots.

"It's magical, isn't it, Hugo?" Marty said.

And it was. The airfield's lights twinkled like stars. Up, up, up they rose. And then, *vroom*, the four engines rumbled to life, and they began to

streak forward through the sky. Hugo felt like a fairy-tale giant. He flew over his kingdom of doll-size houses and churches and matchstick forests.

Gertie turned to Hugo, her face glowing with wonder. And for the first time in months she laughed. The singsong giggle rushed into Hugo's heart and swept away his worries and fears. And for that moment, at least, Hugo let himself believe he really was the luckiest kid on the planet.

CHAPTER 6

THE NEXT DAY
TUESDAY, MAY 4
1:00 P.M.
ABOARD THE *HINDENBURG*

Hugo helped himself to another warm roll, which was as fluffy as the clouds out the window. He'd already eaten four, but nobody seemed to mind. That morning he'd stuffed himself at breakfast — creamy eggs and sizzling sausages. This lunch was even more delicious. The tender steak practically melted on his tongue.

The asparagus was covered with so much melted cheese it actually tasted good.

The family was sharing a big table with Marty and her dad, Mr. Singer, and a few other passengers. Hugo sat next to Marty. Had they met only yesterday? He felt like they'd been friends for years.

Last night they'd stayed up past midnight, looking out the windows. The zeppelin's powerful searchlight beamed down. It lit up sleeping villages and turned the Rhine River into a glittering silver ribbon.

Marty told Hugo about her life with her father.

"My mother died four years ago," she said. "So Father and I are a team."

Hugo had been wondering why she and her dad were traveling alone, and now he had his sad answer.

She asked him a hundred questions about Kenya, and as he answered he could almost see Marty traveling there in her mind. He described their little house with the grass roof, and explained that Mom and Dad took turns giving him his school lessons.

"Are giraffes really the most beautiful animals?" Marty asked.

"Yes, and their eyes are huge, and almost like human eyes," Hugo told her.

There was only one ugly part of a giraffe.

"Their tongues are pitch black, and about a foot and a half long," he added.

"Yuck!" Marty said as they both burst out laughing.

Hugo told Marty about the cobras and the hippos and the one-eared baboon. And then, just before they said good night, he told her the story of Gertie's illness. Marty listened with tears in her eyes.

But today, here in the bright dining room of the *Hindenburg*, those sad stories seemed miles away.

Gertie had woken up without a fever this morning and was gobbling up her food. Mom and Dad looked almost carefree as they chatted with their new friends.

"From now on, I will only travel on zeppelins," announced Miss Crowther. She was an older

American woman with a big voice and even bigger diamond earrings.

Gertie looked up at Hugo, her face shiny with butter from the noodles.

"Oogo," she whispered. "That lady looks like an ostrich."

"You're right, Gertie," he whispered back, studying Miss Crowther's unusually long neck and thin, beaklike nose. "But keep your voice down." He was pretty sure the elegant Miss Crowther wouldn't like being compared to an enormous screeching bird.

"I'm usually sick as a dog on a ship," boomed Mr. Merrick, a British man with red hair and a pointy chin. "But I haven't been the least bit queasy."

Same with Hugo. On the ship to Africa last year, Hugo had been so slammed by seasickness he'd puked his guts out. But the *Hindenburg*'s ride was so smooth. It was impossible to imagine that they were really zooming through the sky at almost eighty-five miles per hour. Hugo's stomach felt perfect.

Gertie studied Mr. Merrick.

"He looks like a fox," she whispered.

Marty grinned — she wanted in on the game.

They all now turned their attention to Mr. Lenz. He was a cheerful German man with a thick, curving mustache and big, pillowy belly.

"I once flew on an airplane," he said. "But never again. The noise was terrible. We had to land every two hours to get more fuel. And it took us twenty-two hours to fly from New York to Florida!"

Hugo had always wanted to fly on an airplane, but he'd heard they were dangerous. Dad said it would be years before an airplane could fly passengers across the oceans. For now, only the *Graf Zeppelin* and the *Hindenburg* could do that.

"Mr. Lenz looks like a nice walrus," Marty whispered.

Gertie giggled, and Hugo and Marty hid their laughing faces behind their fancy linen napkins.

But their game was cut short when suddenly Mr. Lenz's knife clattered noisily onto his plate. Hugo looked up and then followed Mr. Lenz's alarmed gaze to the front of the dining room. Three Nazi officers were standing there, like the men Hugo had seen at the airport. They were all wearing bloodred swastika armbands and had big Luger pistols hanging from their belts.

Mr. Lenz leaned forward. "I recognize that tall man in front," he whispered. "That's Colonel Joseph Kohl. He's known to be a vicious Nazi. Very close to Hitler."

"He's coming over!" Miss Crowther said, her eyes bugging out.

Mr. Singer stood up.

"Colonel Kohl," Mr. Singer said, shaking the Nazi's hand. "I had no idea you were on board."

"We are staying in the officers' quarters in front," the Nazi replied with a sharp German accent. "I was called to New York City for a meeting. What better way to travel than on our glorious zeppelin?"

Hugo tried not to stare at the man, but he couldn't stop himself.

Kohl's white-blond hair was slicked back. He had icy blue eyes and a small, flat nose that sat above thin lips. As he spoke, his small teeth glistened.

Gertie turned to Hugo and pointed at Kohl with an excited grin.

"Oogo," she gasped, forgetting to whisper. "That man looks like a big cobra!"

CHAPTER 7

Nobody at the table seemed to breathe.

Had his little sister really called a Nazi colonel a deadly snake?

Hugo edged closer to Gertie, ready to grab her for a quick escape.

But to Hugo's shock, Kohl smiled.

"Well, thank you, *Liebchen*," he said, reaching out to touch Gertie's cheek with his black-gloved hand. "I am most fascinated by snakes."

Mom stood up and whisked Gertie out of her seat.

"Poor baby is exhausted," she said with a nervous smile. In a flash, they disappeared from the dining room.

Kohl stood there a moment, not seeming to mind the nervous silence.

"I look forward to seeing you all again," he said finally. And with a bow he turned and walked back to where his men were waiting.

Everyone at the table seemed to exhale with relief as the Nazis left the dining room.

"Such an odd man!" Miss Crowther said, reaching for a drink of water.

"What on earth is he doing on the *Hindenburg*?" demanded Mr. Lenz.

Mr. Merrick looked around, alert for eavesdroppers. "I believe Kohl is searching for a spy."

Marty and Hugo looked at each other with wide eyes.

A spy!

"Someone stole a top secret document from the Nazis," Mr. Merrick continued. "It contains a list of Nazis living secretly in America hatching dangerous plots against the United States. The spy has smuggled this paper onto the *Hindenburg* so he can take it to the American government."

"And how do you know this?" Mr. Lenz said.

"I have some important friends," Mr. Merrick said. "That is all I can say."

"That spy must be a courageous man," Dad said.

"Or woman," said Miss Crowther, raising her pointy eyebrows.

"Actually, the Nazis do believe this spy is a man," Mr. Merrick said.

Dad turned to Mr. Singer.

"What do you think?"

Mr. Singer looked thoughtful for a moment.

"I think the *Hindenburg* would be a dangerous place for a spy," he said. "A large ocean liner would be far better. A person can blend in with thousands of passengers and could easily remain hidden."

Hugo had to agree. The ship to Africa had been huge and crowded. Just getting from the dining room to their cabin took fifteen minutes. Hugo once got so lost he was sure he'd never find his family again.

"And how would a spy get secret papers past the guards at the airport?" Mr. Singer asked.

Another good point, Hugo thought. *Who could forget that long line at the Frankfurt airport?*

Miss Crowther's pointy eyebrows rose up even higher.

"Perhaps there's a ghost on the *Hindenburg,* too," she said wryly.

"Or a vampire," chuckled Mr. Lenz.

Mr. Merrick frowned.

"I don't think this is funny," he said. "If there is a spy on this airship, I fear for his life. Kohl will surely catch him before we get to America. He'll lock him up somewhere on this zeppelin and bring him back to Germany."

He looked around.

"Or he'll shoot him on the spot!"

"Mr. Merrick, please!" Miss Crowther scolded. "You're going to give us nightmares."

Miss Crowther was right.

That night, Hugo had a dream that he found a cobra in his bed, a cobra with pale blue eyes and bloodred stripes. But this time Panya wasn't there to chase it away, and the cobra grew and grew, its angry hood flaring into a pair of enormous, slithery wings. The hideous snake smiled at Hugo with yellow fangs dripping with venom.

Hugo woke up in a sweat, gripping his throat.

And it was a long time before he fell asleep again.

CHAPTER 8

THE NEXT DAY
WEDNESDAY, MAY 5

All morning, Hugo and Marty kept their ears pricked up for whispers about the spy. They watched for Colonel Kohl. But the hours passed calmly with no sign of the Nazi.

After lunch, Mom took Gertie back to the cabin for a nap, and Mr. Singer announced that he had a surprise for Hugo and Dad — a tour of the zeppelin.

Of course, Marty came along. They started in the front of the zeppelin, in the *Hindenburg*'s control car.

The airship's command center was just a quick walk from the passenger area, through a short tunnel and then up a few stairs. When Hugo walked in, he had no idea where to look first — at the five men in crisp blue uniforms, at the rows of spinning dials and gauges and levers and buttons, or at the dazzling view of the ocean stretched out as far as he could see.

They shook hands with the *Hindenburg*'s commander, Captain Pruss, a short man who looked more like a kindly science teacher than a famous zeppelin captain. The captain showed them a large map hanging on the wall. He traced the *Hindenburg*'s route across the North Atlantic with his finger, and showed them exactly where they were now.

They were close to land, Hugo could see.

In just a few hours, they'd reach Canada's coast. From there they'd turn south and fly along the

FRANKFURT, GERMANY
ay 3-6,1937-4,389 Miles
ATLANTIC
OCEAN

beaches of New England, over New York City, and finally to the *Hindenburg*'s American airfield, in Lakehurst, New Jersey.

Hugo realized that the voyage was nearly over. Tomorrow morning they'd be landing. He should have felt happy that they were almost back in New York. But part of him didn't want this journey to end. Maybe Marty was right, and there was something magical about the *Hindenburg*. It was almost as though the zeppelin had transported them to another universe, one where Gertie was well and Mom and Dad were happy. And what about Marty? Would he ever see her again?

They said good-bye to Captain Pruss and the others and headed back into the passenger area. But the tour wasn't over. Now Mr. Singer led them down a hallway to a door that was guarded by a young member of the *Hindenburg*'s crew.

The man greeted Mr. Singer with a smile and stepped aside to let them through.

"Passengers aren't allowed into this part of the airship on their own," Mr. Singer said.

As they climbed up into the zeppelin's enormous main body, Hugo had the feeling he'd been swallowed up by a giant animal, with bones and guts made out of bright metal. Thousands of metal beams and girders and wires jutted in every direction. And all around them were huge tan bags — the gas cells filled with hydrogen. They billowed softly, as if they were breathing. If the metal beams were the *Hindenburg*'s bones, these bags of gas were its lungs.

Mr. Singer led them along a narrow walkway that ran straight through the entire body of the airship. He pointed out a row of large tanks. They were filled with water, Mr. Singer explained. The water was used as ballast, extra weight to keep the ship on the ground. When the ship took off, thousands of gallons of water would splash out through the bottom. This made the ship lighter, so it would rise up.

"Remind me not to stand under a zeppelin without an umbrella," Dad laughed.

As they walked farther back, the roar of the engines got louder and louder. Up front in the passenger area, they could barely hear the engines. But back here, the clattering roar hammered against Hugo's eardrums.

And then there was a new sound, a strange growling noise that rose up above the engines.

"What on earth is that?" Mr. Singer said, looking around with worried eyes. "Could that be one of the engines?"

Hugo felt a stab of fear.

"Father, is something wrong?" Marty asked worriedly.

Mr. Singer stood very still. "I've never heard anything like this on a zeppelin. And it doesn't sound right at all."

Mr. Singer turned and hurried over to a big wooden telephone that was mounted to the wall.

He picked up the handle and pushed a button.

"I must notify Captain Pruss immediately!"

CHAPTER 9

The sound got louder.

"*Garooooo! Garooooo! Garooooo!*"

Wait! Hugo had heard that sound before.

It was Panya!

"That's our dog!" Hugo exclaimed.

His howling barks were echoing from farther back in the ship.

Mr. Singer cocked his head and listened.

"Heavens, that dog has a loud bark," Mr. Singer said. "It's louder than the *Hindenburg*'s engines!"

"Can we go see the dog, Father?" Marty asked. "He sounds so lonely!"

Mr. Singer shook his head.

"I wish we could," Mr. Singer said. "But he's in the very back of the zeppelin, and only crew members are permitted back there. Even I'm not allowed in the cargo area."

"Panya's a tough little guy," Dad said, putting his arm around Hugo. "And we'll get to see him tomorrow."

They made their way to the front of the zeppelin. As they walked, Dad eyed the gas cells that wavered all around them.

"How much hydrogen is on this zeppelin?" Dad asked.

"There are sixteen gas cells. Altogether there are seven million cubic feet of gas."

Hugo wasn't an expert, but that seemed like a huge amount.

"I have to ask," Dad said. "Isn't it terribly dangerous to be flying with all of this flammable hydrogen?"

"The gas cells are constantly monitored," Mr. Singer said. "There are ladders and walkways that allow the crew to inspect the cells from every side. The captain has instruments in the cockpit that immediately detect if there is a leak. We've been flying with hydrogen for fourteen years without an accident."

"But still, wouldn't it be wiser to use a safer gas like helium?"

"Of course," Mr. Singer said. "You could throw a torch into a bag of helium and it wouldn't burn. But all of the world's helium comes from the United States. And with Hitler in power, the U.S. government won't sell helium to German companies."

"Not even to make the *Hindenburg* safer?" Dad asked.

Mr. Singer shook his head.

"But I don't understand," Marty said. "Americans love the *Hindenburg*."

Hugo didn't get it, either. Why would the American government worry about zeppelins?

As usual, Dad had an explanation.

"The first German zeppelins were used as weapons," Dad said. "They used them during the Great War."

Hugo's grandfather had fought in that terrible, bloody first world war, which is why Hugo knew all about it. Germany started the war in 1914. Soon the Germans were battling against a team of countries known as the Allies: Great Britain, France, Russia, Italy, and Japan. The United States entered the war in 1917 and helped the Allies defeat Germany.

Never in history had there been such brutal killing in a war. For the first time, soldiers had modern weapons like machine guns and tanks and powerful bombs. There were tremendous battles that killed tens of thousands of men in a single day. The Germans even invented a new kind of weapon, a poison called mustard gas. It killed soldiers by burning their lungs when they breathed, or made them blind.

But Hugo never knew the Germans had used zeppelins, too.

"They used them to drop bombs on England and France," Dad said.

"And you think Hitler would turn the *Hindenburg* into a weapon?" Hugo asked.

Hugo looked around trying to imagine how many bombs the Germans would fit in this enormous space.

Dad and Mr. Singer shared a dark look.

"Hitler is a madman," Mr. Singer said. His voice was very soft, but his friendly eyes now blazed with anger. "Anything is possible."

Just then they heard footsteps rushing toward them, and a man calling out for Mr. Singer.

"Herr Singer! Herr Singer!"

One of the *Hindenburg*'s stewards appeared, red-faced and out of breath.

He glanced at Dad and spoke to Mr. Singer in German.

Hugo could see from Mr. Singer's face that this time something really was wrong — very wrong.

Terrifying thoughts flooded Hugo's mind.

Had Kohl caught the spy?

Was there trouble with the zeppelin?

But then Mr. Singer turned to Dad.

"Mr. Ballard, your wife needs you to come. back to the cabin right away."

Dad went pale.

And somehow Hugo understood.

It wasn't the *Hindenburg* that was in danger.

It was Gertie.

"I'm sorry," Mr. Singer said to Dad. "But it seems your daughter is very sick."

CHAPTER 10

The next few hours went by in a nightmarish blur.

Gertie's fever had spiked to 105 degrees. The ship's doctor, Dr. Rudinger, was trying everything to cool her off, but nothing was working.

And the worst part was that Hugo wasn't allowed into the cabin. He and Dad had to wait in the hallway while the doctor and Mom took care of Gertie.

Day turned to night, and Hugo lost all sense of time.

He prayed and tried to calm himself with his favorite memories — seeing the Yankees beat the

Red Sox, walking through the bright green hills of the Thika Valley after a strong rain, sharing a mango with the one-eared baboon. But those happy pictures would flicker and fade. And all Hugo could think about was his little sister, lying pale and still in her bed.

And then he couldn't think at all. His mind filled up with a terrible clawing fear, as if a big black bird were trapped inside his skull.

It was very early in the morning when Dr. Rudinger finally stepped out of their cabin.

"She's stable now," he told them. "We finally got her fever down."

Hugo almost fainted with relief.

Dad grabbed the doctor's hands. "Thank you, Doctor."

"We'll have an ambulance waiting at the airfield when we land."

Dad looked at his watch.

"Thank goodness," Dad said. "We land at six A.M. That's only three hours from now."

The doctor shook his head. "No, sir. There have been strong headwinds across the Atlantic.

And now there are storms all along the East Coast. We're running at least eight hours behind schedule."

Eight hours?

Hugo's knees went weak, and Dad looked like he might get sick.

The doctor put a hand on Dad's shoulder. "Your little girl is very tough, Mr. Ballard."

He promised to check back within the hour.

Hugo and Dad went into their cabin. Gertie was sleeping, and Mom was sitting by her bed. Mom looked like she'd just returned from a back-breaking journey.

Mom got up and hugged Hugo.

"Can I sit with her?" Hugo asked.

"Of course."

"I'll take your mother to stretch her legs," Dad said. "We'll be back in a few minutes."

Hugo sat in the chair and laid a careful hand on his sister's forehead. She still felt hot, but not like she was burning up.

He knew he should let her sleep. But he needed to hear her voice.

"Gertie," Hugo whispered. "It's me."

Gertie's eyes fluttered open.

"Oogo," she rasped.

Their eyes locked together.

Some invisible evil was attacking his sister, and Hugo could do nothing to help her.

I'm sorry, Hugo wanted to say, *sorry that I can't protect you.*

He'd never felt more helpless.

He leaned closer to Gertie, taking her hand.

"Gertie," he said. "Is there anything you want?"

If she'd wanted the moon, Hugo would have climbed out the window and ripped it out of the sky for her.

But his sister didn't want the moon.

She looked at Hugo.

"Panya," she whimpered.

Gertie wanted her dog.

CHAPTER 11

When Mom and Dad came back, Hugo told them he was going out to the big windows to get some fresh air. But instead, he made his way down to the lower deck. He followed the route that they'd taken with Mr. Singer earlier.

He was going to sneak into the cargo area and get Panya.

The hallways were quiet, but Hugo heard voices whispering from some of the rooms. Twice he had to duck behind corners to avoid being spotted by members of the crew. But luckily there was no guard posted in front of the door leading out of the passenger area. He managed to slip through without getting caught.

The inside of the airship's body was very dark, and it took a moment for Hugo's eyes to adjust. Earlier, the light of the sun had shone through the *Hindenburg*'s skin, giving the interior a bright glow. But now the air looked inky black. The few bulbs hanging from the girders cast a ghostly light.

Hugo swallowed hard and headed down the narrow walkway until the noises of the engines pounded in his ears. He kept walking toward the very back of the zeppelin. He passed a very big sign with the angry-looking words:

ZUTRITT VERBOTEN

Hugo was pretty sure that meant something like *keep out*.

He was in the cargo area now, surrounded by shelves piled high with trunks and crates. Above him, the gas bags whispered quietly.

And then a familiar sound:

"Garoo, garoo, garoo!"

Panya must have smelled Hugo coming, and now Hugo just had to follow the howls. He walked to the very back, and there was a big wicker cage. Hugo popped open the door and Panya leaped into his arms.

The little dog's tail whipped back and forth. Hugo stood there for a moment, nuzzling his dog, happily accepting a shower of slobbering licks.

"Gertie needs you," Hugo whispered. "And now you have to stay very quiet."

Panya looked at Hugo, his eyes suddenly alert.

Let's go, he seemed to say.

But before they'd even made it out of the cargo area, Hugo heard footsteps.

Someone was coming!

He ducked behind a large wooden crate, tucking Panya into his shirt.

"Shhh," he warned.

Peeking up, Hugo could see the shadowy shape of a man heading toward them.

Hugo figured it was a member of the crew on a nightly inspection.

But as the man got closer, Hugo could see a fuzzy puff of hair and the glint of round glasses.

It was Mr. Singer!

Hugo almost jumped up. Mr. Singer must be looking for Hugo. He wanted to help him find Panya!

But wait.

Hugo had told nobody about his plan to sneak back here. So how would Mr. Singer have known to come looking?

And if he wasn't coming to help Hugo, what was Mr. Singer doing in this forbidden area of the zeppelin? He'd said himself that not even he was allowed in this rear cargo area.

The hairs on Hugo's arms prickled as he watched Mr. Singer study the shelves. Finally, Mr. Singer stopped at a large wooden box. He lifted the lid and rummaged inside. Moments later, he pulled out a large envelope.

In the low light, Hugo could just make out a huge swastika stamped onto the front.

And words in big block letters.

STRENG GEHEIM!

Again, even without knowing German, Hugo understood. Whatever was inside that envelope was important.

Hugo's whole body tingled as it suddenly dawned on him.

Marty's father was the spy.

CHAPTER 12

Marty's father!

It seemed crazy, until it made perfect sense.

Everyone on the *Hindenburg* trusted Mr. Singer. He knew his way all around the zeppelin. He had probably been allowed to skip the inspections at the airport. And he even acted friendly with Colonel Kohl. Nobody would suspect that smiling Mr. Singer was actually a courageous spy. Which made him perfect for the job.

But then Hugo's amazement turned to fear as voices echoed from the front of the zeppelin.

And there was no mistaking the sharp hissing voice that rose up louder than the others.

It was Kohl.

Mr. Singer's eyes scanned all around. And then he caught sight of Hugo, and his eyes grew wide with shock. But quickly the look seemed to change.

I need your help, Mr. Singer seemed to say.

The sound of footsteps and threatening voices got louder and louder.

Mr. Singer tucked the envelope under his arm and rushed over to the ladder. It reached up into the gas cells, and then to a walkway that led to the front of the ship.

But the ladder was so tall. Mr. Singer would never make it up in time!

Colonel Kohl would catch him. And then what?

Hugo remembered Mr. Merrick's chilling warning.

That spy will be shot on the spot!

A wave of fear crashed over Hugo, nearly knocking him down.

He crouched lower.

61

He felt small and helpless, the way he felt when he was sitting by Gertie's bed, watching her get burned up by those terrible fevers.

He couldn't help Gertie. And there was nothing he could do to help Mr. Singer.

But then Hugo's mind suddenly flashed to his friend, the one-eared baboon.

Hugo remembered watching the baboon at the watering hole one day.

There was a giant hippo, and it was terrorizing any animal that dared try to get close.

But the baboon figured out how to distract the hippo. He threw rocks to the other side of the watering hole, where it was too muddy to drink. When the hippo got up to investigate, the baboon rushed over to slurp up a big refreshing helping of water.

By the time the hippo turned around, the baboon was long gone.

Hugo thought for a moment, suddenly inspired.

No, he couldn't stop Kohl searching for the spy.

But maybe Hugo could distract Kohl so he wouldn't spot Mr. Singer on the ladder.

Before he knew for sure that he had the courage, Hugo was on his feet. Panya wriggled out of Hugo's shirt and stood tall in his arms, ready for anything.

Just then Kohl appeared out of the darkness, trailed by the two Nazi officers and four members of the *Hindenburg*'s crew.

"Halt!" he barked.

In one hand Kohl held a bright flashlight, which beamed blindingly into their eyes.

In the other he held his Luger pistol, which he aimed at Hugo's heart.

CHAPTER 13

"What are you doing here?" Kohl hissed. "It is forbidden for you to be in this part of the zeppelin."

"I'm sorry," Hugo answered, his voice shaking. "My sister is sick, sir. She wanted to see our dog. I came to get him. I know it's against the rules."

Kohl took a step closer, and Panya began to growl menacingly.

"Rrrrrrrrrrrrr."

Panya only made that noise when he saw cobras or scented a leopard or some other dangerous beast that could threaten Hugo or Gertie. Hugo didn't doubt that given the chance, the dog would attach its jaws to Kohl's throat.

"Silence that wretched little *Hund*," the Nazi thundered. "Or I will have it thrown from the zeppelin."

Hugo pulled Panya closer into his chest.

"A crew member reported that he saw a man back here," Kohl said. "It is urgent that we find him. This man is very dangerous."

Somehow Hugo managed to look Kohl right in the eye.

"There is no one back here, sir," Hugo said softly. "Only me."

Kohl inched closer to Hugo.

"You know, young man, I can always tell if a person is lying. A liar's sweat gives off a stench, like rotting flesh."

He leaned in, putting his nose close to Hugo's face. He sniffed.

Panya growled, but Hugo held him back.

Maybe this Nazi really did have the power to sniff out a lie. Some animals could smell fear, Hugo knew.

But Hugo hadn't lied, not really.

Mr. Singer wasn't here. Not anymore.

"The man we are looking for is a filthy criminal," Kohl said. "He is a traitor. Anyone caught helping this man will be arrested."

"I'm telling the truth, sir," Hugo said, his voice more steady now. "You can come with me to see my parents. The doctor has been with my sister for hours."

Colonel Kohl kept his icy eyes on Hugo. But now Hugo could see it — the unmistakable look of disappointment on the Nazi's face.

Kohl hadn't caught the spy.

He'd caught a boy with his dog.

And by now the real spy was on his way back to the passenger area.

"Don't let me see you back here again," Kohl warned. "If I do, I will lock you up."

Then he ordered one of the crew members to take Hugo back to his cabin.

Mom and Dad stared in shock when Hugo walked in with Panya.

He went straight over to Gertie.

Without a word, he put Panya down on the bed.

Gertie opened her eyes and gasped.

And then she looked at Hugo as if he really had brought her the moon.

Her face became more peaceful as Panya snuggled up to her.

Hugo watched as his sister drifted off to sleep.

"Hugo, how?" Mom said.

"Did Mr. Singer help you?" Dad said.

Hugo nodded but said nothing more. He knew he couldn't tell Mom and Dad what he'd seen. If Mr. Singer got caught, and Kohl figured out that Mom and Dad knew the truth, they could be arrested — or worse.

Hugo climbed into bed next to his sister and their dog, wrapping his arms around both of them. He was done thinking for now.

The worst was over, he told himself.

Later that morning, the *Hindenburg* would land.

And nothing more could go wrong.

CHAPTER 14

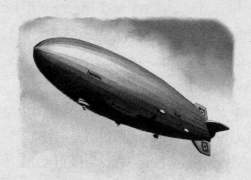

THE NEXT MORNING
THURSDAY, MAY 6

Overnight, the weather had turned dark and stormy. The *Hindenburg* flew down the coast of New England through a tunnel of thick gray clouds. The patter of rain sounded like a million rocks pounding against the zeppelin.

But the mood was brighter inside their cabin because Gertie had woken up without a fever. As they were getting dressed for breakfast, there was a knock on the cabin door. Hugo's heart dropped into his stomach.

What if it was Colonel Kohl coming to arrest him, and Mom and Dad, too?

What if he'd caught Mr. Singer?

But Mom opened the door, and Hugo almost fainted with happiness at the sight of Mr. Singer and Marty.

Marty rushed over to hug Gertie, and to meet Panya. She didn't notice the long look Hugo and Mr. Singer shared. With that one look, Mr. Singer managed to tell Hugo he was safe.

For now.

Gertie felt well enough to go to breakfast, and Panya didn't whimper too much when they left him in the cabin. The whole dining room seemed to light up when Gertie walked in. They sat with their friends, and the usual lively chatter rose up around them.

But all Hugo could think about was Colonel Kohl. The Nazi had stalked his prey to the cargo room last night. He had lost the trail. But Kohl would not give up.

Mr. Singer was still in terrible danger. He wouldn't be safe until he was off the *Hindenburg*.

Hugo just wanted this zeppelin to land.

But the stormy weather slowed them down, and the hours dragged on.

Hugo passed the time with Gertie and Marty in the lounge. At noon they flew over Boston, but it was so cloudy Hugo barely got a glimpse of Fenway Park.

By 3:00 P.M. they'd made it to New York City, and the clouds cleared. The ship dipped down so they could see the 102-story Empire State Building, the tallest building in the world. They could actually see people waving to them from the building's observation deck.

Lakehurst, New Jersey, was a short distance from New York City, and hopes rose that the zeppelin would finally be able to land. Packed suitcases lined the hallways. Some passengers even put on their coats. But then word came that a new line of thunderstorms had rolled in, and that landing would be too dangerous.

The zeppelin zoomed away from New York City and back out to sea. Mom brought Gertie to the cabin to nap with Panya. And for hours Hugo and Marty sat together as the zeppelin circled slowly over the New Jersey coast. Thunder rumbled all around them, and they could see the huge waves pounding angrily against the shore.

It was close to 7:00 P.M. when the skies finally started to clear, and rays of sun broke through the clouds. Hugo felt the airship turn sharply and then gain speed.

"I think we're going to land!" Marty said.

And sure enough, within just a few minutes, the Lakehurst airfield came into view.

Hugo spotted an enormous building — the *Hindenburg*'s hangar. Beyond it was a big open field where the landing crew was already waiting. There must have been at least two hundred men.

Meanwhile the lounge was filling up with passengers. People lined up at the windows, just as they had three days ago when the *Hindenburg* took off.

Mr. Singer appeared.

"You should get your family," he said to Hugo. "We'll be on the ground within minutes."

They shared a smile, and a feeling of relief washed over Hugo. But it didn't last long.

Because just then a voice called out.

"Herr Singer!"

Hugo whipped around.

Kohl was walking toward them with the other two Nazi officers.

He looked at Mr. Singer.

"Herr Singer, could you join us in the control car? Captain Pruss has asked for you."

Hugo's guts turned to jelly.

But Mr. Singer remained calm.

"I'll be delighted to see the captain after we land," he said.

Kohl stepped forward.

"I'm afraid it's urgent," he said coldly.

He pulled his gun from his belt.

Marty screamed.

And then,

Kaboom!

CHAPTER 15

But the blast had not come from Kohl's pistol.

It seemed to have come from somewhere above, somewhere deep within the zeppelin.

Kohl himself looked startled — and confused.

Had the zeppelin been struck by lightning?

Hugo looked out the windows, but he saw no clouds.

What he could see were the faces of the men standing on the ground. They were gaping at the *Hindenburg*, their eyes wide with shock and horror. Some of the ground crew were actually sprinting away, as if they were running for their lives.

And then came a violent jerk. The tail of the zeppelin suddenly dropped down, dumping Hugo and everyone else onto the floor. They all went sliding back, a wave of frantic people rolling down the sloping floor. Elbows jabbed at Hugo. A sharp heel kicked his forehead. Someone's knee pressed so hard on his neck he couldn't breathe. He wound up against the back wall, mashed behind at least ten bodies and a jumble of overturned tables and chairs.

He squirmed and rolled and pushed until he freed himself from the heap.

But he had barely caught his breath when he glanced up toward the ceiling and saw something that made his blood freeze. It was a sight more terrifying than a cobra coiled in his bed or even a Nazi with a pistol.

It was fire.

Fire on an airship filled with millions of cubic feet of flammable hydrogen gas.

And then, with a thundering *whoosh*, the room exploded into flames.

The blast of searing heat knocked Hugo back.

His head hit the floor with a sickening thud. Oily black smoke rushed up his nose and down his throat.

Hugo gagged and coughed.

His mind screamed in panic, *Get out! Get out! Get out!*

In just seconds, the *Hindenburg* would burst into a giant ball of flames.

Where were Mom and Dad and Gertie?

People were running out of the lounge, screaming and shouting.

"Hurry!"

"We're crashing!"

"It's the end!"

Hugo felt as if he were caught in a stampede.

Then someone grabbed Hugo by the back of his jacket and freed him from the crushing crowd. It was Mr. Singer, with Marty right behind him.

Hugo had lost sight of them, but now Marty clamped hold of his hand as though she'd never let go. Hugo hoped she never would.

Mr. Singer looked frantically around.

"This way," he said, pushing them both back toward the windows.

"Sir, I have to find my family!" Hugo said.

"They'll find a way out, Hugo. And they'd want you to get out, too. There isn't any time."

Mr. Singer grabbed a toppled chair. "Duck!" he called out as he swung the chair up and smashed it against the windows.

The glass shattered.

They were close to the ground, Hugo could see, about fifteen feet up. Scraps of burning fabric filled the sky. It looked as if it were raining fire. He could see that some people from the zeppelin had already escaped. Sailors from the crew were braving the flames to help them get away.

A young sailor stood just below them, looking up with open arms.

"Jump!" he cried. "Hurry!"

Mr. Singer helped Marty climb up to the window ledge.

"Go! We'll be right behind you!"

Marty took one last look at Hugo and her father.

Then she closed her eyes and leaped.

The sailor caught her and ran away carrying her in his arms.

"Your turn!" Mr. Singer shouted to Hugo.

But just then a dark shape appeared from out of the smoke.

It was Kohl!

Hugo had been right. Nothing was going to stop Kohl from finding his prey.

And now he really did look like a vicious predator.

There was blood dripping from a gash in his cheek. His eyes looked almost bright red — like his fury was boiling inside him.

Kohl pointed his pistol at Mr. Singer. This time Hugo had no doubt he was going to shoot.

"I know what you did!" Kohl bellowed, his voice rising up above the crackling fire and the groaning of the airship. "Hand the papers over to me now!"

Mr. Singer backed up until he was pressed against the wall.

The zeppelin was shaking now, the flames churning all around them. It was almost impossible to breathe.

With every second that went by, their chance to escape slipped further away.

And then Hugo heard a terrifying noise.

He looked up just in time to see a metal beam crashing through the ceiling — and it was heading right for them!

CHAPTER 16

The beam came down like a flaming sword.

Hugo fell back and rolled onto his side, bracing for the deadly crack of metal on his head. But the beam just missed him.

It had missed Mr. Singer, too.

But Colonel Kohl wasn't so lucky. The beam had landed across his neck. He lay there with his eyes open, motionless, his hand still gripping his gun.

Hugo could see that Colonel Kohl wouldn't ever be getting up again.

But there was no time for Hugo to think about this. The airship was falling and breaking apart.

His lungs felt as though they would explode. He and Mr. Singer both jumped up. They joined hands and lunged for the windows.

Mr. Singer heaved Hugo out first.

The zeppelin was so close to the ground that Hugo barely felt the impact. He landed on his stomach. Seconds later, Mr. Singer landed a few feet away.

Hugo got up and turned to run.

But something hit his back — hard.

And he suddenly realized it was too late.

Chunks of the flaming *Hindenburg* were now crashing down around Hugo and Mr. Singer — the white-hot metal beams. The slabs of burning walls.

Men shouted to them.

"Hurry! Get up! Get up!"

There was fire everywhere now — raining from the sky, rising from the ground, burning his clothes, his shoes, his hair.

Hugo dropped to the ground and curled into a ball.

There was no hope.

His body erupted in scorching pain as the fire raked his flesh. And then Hugo couldn't feel anything. His mind went dark, his breathing stopped.

But suddenly his brain flickered back to life, and Hugo felt sure that somehow he'd been dropped out of the burning *Hindenburg* and into the Thika River. Cool water rushed all around him.

The next thing he knew he was lying on a soft blanket, with bright lights all around. Was he back in Kenya, under the golden sun?

He heard voices calling for him:

"Hugo!"

"Hugo!"

"Oogo!"

And the loudest of all, *"Garooo, garooo, garooo!"*

CHAPTER 17

SIX WEEKS LATER
SUNDAY, JUNE 20
FITKIN MEMORIAL HOSPITAL
NEPTUNE, NEW JERSEY

Hugo opened his eyes. It was just getting light out, and he listened for the familiar sounds of a Kenyan morning — shrieking monkeys and cawing birds and buzzing insects.

Instead Hugo heard hushed voices and footsteps.

No, he realized. He wasn't in Kenya.

He was still in the hospital, in New Jersey.

But finally today, after forty-five days, he was going home.

The burns on his back were finally healing. The wounds still hurt. And Hugo had a big bald patch on the side of his head. The doctors couldn't say for sure whether the hair would grow back. But the worst was behind him. That's what everyone told him.

But was it really? Hugo wasn't sure.

Hugo couldn't wait to get out of the hospital.

He missed Gertie — kids weren't allowed to visit. He missed Panya, too. And of course Marty, who had written to him every day.

But part of Hugo was afraid to leave here, to be out in the world again.

He knew that everyone was still talking about the *Hindenburg* disaster.

They'd want to talk to him about it, to hear his story, to share their ideas about what had caused the crash. Nobody knew for sure yet. Some said it was a bomb. Others were convinced it was a gas leak ignited by a spark from the lightning-filled sky.

Hugo didn't want to think about any of that. He just wanted to forget that he was ever on the *Hindenburg*.

He still had nightmares every night, terrible dreams filled with fire and smoke and giant hissing cobras. He'd wake up screaming, until the nurses rushed in with their hushed voices and comforting hands.

Even during the day, terror would grab hold of him, out of nowhere. He'd catch a whiff of smoke, or take a bite of a warm roll that Mom and Dad brought for him. And his whole body would start to shake.

He'd think of the thirty-six people who had died in the crash, like Mr. Merrick. He'd think of Mr. Singer, whose burns were even worse than Hugo's.

He'd think about how scared Gertie must have been when Mom dropped her out the dining room window into the arms of a man from the crew. He'd picture Mom leaping out with Miss Crowther, and breaking her wrist as she landed.

And worst of all was thinking about Dad, who had stayed behind to search for Hugo. He'd rushed through the burning zeppelin calling Hugo's name until Mr. Lenz had dragged him away from the flames and pushed him through a burned-out hole in the wall.

And what had happened to Hugo? How had he and Mr. Singer escaped from the burning field of wreckage?

It turned out one of the *Hindenburg*'s huge water tanks had hit the ground and burst open. Thousands of gallons of water had gushed out. The cool waters had washed over Hugo and Mr. Singer, dousing the flames that threatened to kill them both. During the brief moments when the fires died down, two brave men from the ground crew had rushed in and carried them off the airfield.

Mr. Singer was in bad shape. But he was getting better, too. He was at a different hospital, but Marty gave him reports in the letters she sent. She was staying with her grandparents in Boston until her father was better.

At least Hugo didn't have to keep Mr. Singer's secret, because it wasn't a secret anymore.

Dad had showed Hugo a long article in the *New York Times* about how a heroic man named Peter Singer had smuggled secret Nazi documents onto the *Hindenburg*. The papers listed the names of twenty dangerous German spies living secretly in the U.S. The spies reported to Colonel Joseph Kohl, who had died on the *Hindenburg*. By now, all of the spies had been captured.

Marty said that she and her father had even been invited to meet President Roosevelt.

Later that morning, Mom and Dad came to take Hugo home from the hospital. And there was a surprise for him in the waiting room.

At first Hugo didn't recognize the rosy-cheeked little girl who'd come prancing in.

"Oogo!"

Gertie ran up and flew into Hugo's arms.

Tears sprang into his eyes as Gertie gripped him tight.

But these were happy tears.

Mom and Dad had told Hugo that the new malaria medicine had worked, that within a month of taking the first dose, there were no traces of the disease in Gertie's blood.

But only now did Hugo truly believe that his sister was well.

Gertie reached up and gently touched the bald patch on the side of Hugo's head.

"Oogo," she said. "You look like the baboon."

"Gertie!" Mom scolded.

But Hugo laughed, for the first time since the crash.

"You're right, Gertie," he said. He did look a little like his friend the one-eared baboon. Thinking about that made Hugo strangely happy.

They walked out to the car. They would be heading back to their New York City apartment. They wouldn't be returning to Kenya; Mom and Dad wouldn't risk Gertie getting malaria again. So in September, Hugo would be going back to his old school. His pals had sent him letters and cards, and even a new Yankees pennant signed by Lou Gehrig himself.

Panya was waiting in the car, and he was so excited to see Hugo that he managed to propel

his little body out the window and almost knock Hugo off his feet.

The raggedy little mutt jumped up and down, trying to land a slobbery kiss on Hugo's face.

Gertie's singsong giggle rose up all around them.

Mom and Dad each took one of Hugo's hands, and the three of them stood there watching Gertie with amazement.

Yes, Hugo's little sister was well. And it hit Hugo that their journey on the *Hindenburg* had helped save her.

There really had been some magic on that ship.

Hugo looked up, and for the first time in weeks the sight of the blue sky didn't make him feel afraid.

He remembered the thrill of rising up, up, up.

He could picture the twinkling lights of the peaceful world below.

And he understood he could never let himself forget the feeling of soaring through the clouds on the greatest flying machine ever built.

WOULD YOU WANT TO RIDE ON A ZEPPELIN?

You'd think that after writing about the fiery *Hindenburg* disaster, I'd be having nightmares about zeppelins. But instead, I keep thinking about how absolutely wonderful it must have been to soar through the sky on one of those beautiful flying machines.

I actually knew very little about zeppelins when I started researching this book. I barely even knew the word *zeppelin*, and I thought that they were the same as blimps (which they are not!).

I was familiar with the *Hindenburg* disaster, of course. And I'd seen the Pixar movie *Up*, with the villain and his dogs cruising around in their zeppelin. (Fun fact: That cartoon zeppelin was modeled after the *Hindenburg*'s sister ship, the *Graf Zeppelin*.)

But I had no idea that in the 1930s, tens of thousands of people flew more than a million miles on zeppelins. They'd speed across Europe or over oceans with glorious views of the world below. Unlike today's airplanes, which can fly at an altitude of nearly forty thousand feet, zeppelins flew below the clouds, sometimes just a few hundred feet above the ground. Zeppelin passengers really could see whales and dolphins leaping out of the ocean. Many saw icebergs, like the one that sank the *Titanic*. Flying over cities, they could wave hello to people in skyscrapers.

And what luxury! The food was delicious. The tiny cabins were famous for their comfort. Some of the world's richest and most famous people flew on the *Graf Zeppelin* and the *Hindenburg*, which were in fact the only two zeppelins that could carry paying travelers (other zeppelins were used for military purposes).

No wonder people around the world were fascinated by zeppelins. When the *Hindenburg* made its first flight to America, in 1936, thousands packed the streets of New York City so they could catch a glimpse. American kids played with zeppelin toys. Ladies wore zeppelin pins.

You could even send your friend a zeppelin valentine.

By 1937, many people believed that zeppelins would become as common as trains or ships. It's important to remember that long-distance travel back then was very different than it is today. There weren't highways crisscrossing the country. Airplane travel was brand-new, and planes couldn't yet carry passengers over the oceans (plus they crashed a lot!).

Most people traveled on trains and ships. A journey across the Atlantic took nearly a week, and many people dreaded the days of seasickness that often came with ship travel.

Between 1928 and 1937, the *Graf Zeppelin* and the *Hindenburg* made more than two thousand journeys. They flew across Europe, to America, and between Germany and South America. These two zeppelins were so successful that several American companies were hoping to build airship fleets of their own.

But then came the *Hindenburg* disaster.

In just thirty-two seconds, the most beautiful and sophisticated airship ever built was destroyed.

The disaster was captured on film. Within days, millions of people around the world had watched as the *Hindenburg*'s shimmering silver skin was burned away and the *Titanic*-size airship crashed into a heap of twisted metal and ash. They saw photographs of survivors who had been horribly burned. People lost confidence in zeppelins.

The *Hindenburg* disaster didn't just destroy a great aircraft. It ended the age of zeppelins — forever. Amazingly, nobody ever flew across the ocean on a zeppelin again.

And I can't help feeling sad about that.

The *Hindenburg* disaster might still appear in one of my nightmares. But to me, crossing the ocean in a zeppelin (filled with nonflammable helium, please!) would be a dream come true.

QUESTIONS AND ANSWERS ABOUT THE *HINDENBURG*

What caused the *Hindenburg* to explode?

There are many theories about this. The most sinister is that somebody planted a bomb on the *Hindenburg*. This theory has been used in many movies and books. I even included a bomb in first drafts of *this* book. (I couldn't resist, but in the end that plot point fizzled.)

There really had been bomb threats sent to the Zeppelin Company in the days before the *Hindenburg*'s flight. After the disaster, some of the surviving crew members were convinced that it was an explosive that destroyed their zeppelin.

The problem with this intriguing theory is that it is almost certainly untrue.

In the weeks following the disaster, investigators from the United States and Germany inspected the wreckage. They interviewed surviving passengers and crew. Both teams ruled out a bomb as the cause of the disaster. There have been many studies since, and none have found evidence of a bomb.

Most likely, the disaster was caused by a small hydrogen gas leak in one of the rear gas cells. And this leaking hydrogen was ignited by a spark.

But what caused the spark? This still isn't known for sure. It could have been a loose wire near one of the gas cells. Or, more likely, the thunderstorms left behind static electricity in the air. (You know when you run across a carpet in your socks, and then you touch your brother and he gets a shock? That's an example of static electricity.)

The truth is that we might never know for certain what doomed the *Hindenburg*.

What is certain is that the dangers of hydrogen gas were well known. The Germans took precautions to prevent disaster. But in the end, there was no way to make flying a hydrogen-filled zeppelin perfectly safe.

Was the *Hindenburg* the deadliest zeppelin disaster?

Ever hear of the *Shenandoah*? The *Dixmude*? The *Akron*? These are the names of airships that exploded or crashed in the years before the *Hindenburg*. All of those airship disasters were far more deadly than the crash of the *Hindenburg*.

Altogether, 36 people were killed in the *Hindenburg* crash — 13 passengers (out of 36), 22 crew members (out of 61), and a member of the landing crew.

Given the force of the explosion and crash, many consider it miraculous that so many people survived. The heroic actions of the men on the ground helped. Dozens risked their own lives by rushing to the disaster scene to pull people out of the burning wreckage and to help them to safety.

The deadliest airship disaster was the *Akron*, the U.S. Navy airship that got caught in a thunderstorm off the coast of New Jersey in 1933. The violent winds sent the airship crashing. Of the 76 men on board, 73 drowned.

Is a zeppelin the same as a blimp?

They look similar, but they are quite different. Blimps are more like balloons in that they do not have rigid metal frames. Because of that, they are far less sturdy than zeppelins and not used for travel. Today, blimps are most commonly used to film sporting events. That's why you are most likely to see one hovering over a stadium.

Was Germany's leader Adolf Hitler really dangerous and evil?

Yes.

Adolf Hitler became the leader of Germany in 1933, and almost right away he began building up Germany's army and military might. In 1939, German armies invaded Poland, which started World War II.

Between 1939 and 1945, World War II engulfed Europe and much of the world. It involved more than one hundred countries. America entered the war in 1941 and joined forces with France, Great Britain, the Soviet Union, and other countries such as Canada, Australia, New Zealand, India, and China. This "team" became known as the Allied Powers. (The same term was used in World War I.) The Allies fought against Germany, Japan, and Italy, the main countries among the Axis Powers. The Allied Powers won.

This war that Hitler started killed more than sixty million people, including more than 400,000 American soldiers.

In the years before and during World War II, Hitler also planned and carried out one of history's most evil crimes — the murder of more than six million Jewish people, plus hundreds of thousands of gay people, Roma, and others. This is known as the Holocaust.

Did the Americans really refuse to sell helium to Germany for the *Hindenburg*?

Yes. Many people in the United States were convinced that Hitler was plotting a war and were worried that the Germans could use helium for military purposes. It's also true that Germany used zeppelins for bombing missions in World

War I (which, in 1937, was known as the Great War).

Is it possible to fly on a zeppelin today?

Actually, you can. The *Zeppelin NT* takes tourists on short sightseeing trips around Germany. The flights take off from the *Hindenburg*'s airfield, near Frankfurt. Tickets are roughly $200 for children.

But some people want to bring helium-filled zeppelins back for long-distance travel. Why? Because zeppelins create far less air pollution than jets. In fact, a zeppelin flying from New York City to London puts 90 percent less carbon dioxide into the air than a jet airplane.

Sure, the trip would take much longer than on a commercial jet. But think of the beautiful views!

More *Hindenburg* Facts:

- **SIZE:** 803.8 feet long, 80 feet shorter than the *Titanic* (and about double the length of a football field). It is still the largest object ever to fly.
- **WEIGHT:** Fully loaded, 540,000 tons. It could carry 500,000 pounds.
- **COST:** In 1937, a one-way ticket from Europe to America cost $450, equivalent to about $7,000 in today's dollars.
- **DISTANCE TRAVELED:** The trip from Frankfurt

to Lakehurst, New Jersey, was about four thousand miles.

- **TIME TRAVELED:** Three days. The trip was supposed to take two and a half days. But strong headwinds over the Atlantic and storms along the American coast ended up delaying the airship by twelve hours, a delay that was highly unusual for the Zeppelin Company.

- **SPEED:** The average cruising speed was 76 mph. Maximum speed was 84 mph.

- **PASSENGERS and CREW:** The *Hindenburg* had enough cabin space to carry about 70 passengers; there were only 36 on board on its last voyage, plus 61 officers and crew members.

- **CARGO:** In addition to carrying passengers across the Atlantic Ocean, the *Hindenburg* carried cargo. During its 1936 voyages, it carried cars, a horse, and an antelope for the Cincinnati Zoo.

Want to learn more? Here are some amazing resources to explore.

Airships.net

If you want to take an amazing journey through the history of airships and the *Hindenburg*, this incredible website is for you. Its creator, Dan Grossman, would be flattered to be called the biggest zeppelin geek in the world. His site includes a dizzying amount of information about airships from history and today.

Books

The Disaster of the Hindenburg, by Shelley Tanaka, Toronto, Canada: Madison Press, 1993

Tanaka is one of the best authors of narrative nonfiction I have ever read, and her book interweaves the story of the disaster with that of the *Hindenburg*'s cabin boy, Werner Franz, and a passenger, Irene Boehner. Irene was sixteen at the time and traveling with her parents and two younger brothers. Franz survived the disaster, but Irene did not.

Inside the Hindenburg, by Mirielle Majoor, illustrations by Ken Marschall, New York, NY: Little, Brown, 2000

The information in this book is great, but what will dazzle you are the stunning illustrations. Ken Marschall is a talented artist who also lent his creative powers to beautiful books about the *Titanic.* You will feel like you are walking inside the zeppelin.

The Mzungu Boy, by Meja Mwangi, Toronto, Canada: Groundwood Books, 2006

To imagine Hugo and Gertie's life in Kenya, I read many books about white settlers who lived in Africa in the 1920s and 1930s. But my favorite was this novel for kids your age.

And also:

Two of my I Survived books focus on this time period surrounding World War II:
I Survived the Nazi Invasion, 1944
I Survived the Bombing of Pearl Harbor, 1941

SELECTED BIBLIOGRAPHY

Books and Videos:

Camera Trails in Africa, by Martin Johnson, Torrington, WY: The Narrative Press, 2001

The Flame Trees of Thika: Memories of an African Childhood, paperback reissue, by Elspeth Huxley, New York, NY: Penguin Classics, 2000

The Great Dirigibles: Their Triumphs and Disasters, rev. ed., by John Toland, Mineola, NY: Dover Publications, 1972

Hindenburg: *An Illustrated History*, first American ed., by Rick Archbold, illustrations by Ken Marschall, New York, NY: Warner Books, 1994

Hindenburg's *Fiery Secrets*, documentary DVD, Washington, DC: National Geographic Video, 2010

"I Was on the *Hindenburg*," by Margaret Mathers, *Harper's Magazine*, November 1937, 590–595

Lighter than Air: An Illustrated History of Balloons and Airships, by Tom D. Crouch, Baltimore, MD: Johns Hopkins University Press, 2009

Transatlantic Airships: An Illustrated History, by John Christopher, Ramsbury, Wiltshire, UK: The Crowood Press, 2010

West with the Night, second ed., by Beryl Markham, Berkeley, CA: North Point Press, 2013